Text and illustrations copyright © Shoo Rayner 1999

First published in Great Britain in 1999
by Macdonald Young Books
an imprint of Wayland Publishers Ltd
61 Western Road
Hove
East Sussex
BN3 1JD

Find Macdonald Young Books on the internet at http://www.myb.co.uk

Designed by Triggerfish, 11 Jew Street, Brighton, BN1 1UT
Printed in Hong Kong by Wing King Tong Co. Ltd.

British Library Cataloguing in Publication Data available

ISBN 0 7500 2706 1

SuperDad

The
Super Hero

Shoo Rayner

MACDONALD YOUNG BOOKS

My dad is very busy.
He goes to work early in the morning.
He gets home late at night.

But sometimes he gets home early.
Then he reads me Super Hero stories
before I go to sleep.

The return of
Super Hero

Dad makes the stories really exciting.
He makes all the noises and pretends
that he is Super Hero.

One day Dad was reading the paper.
He said, "Look! Super Hero will be
at the Fun Park on Saturday.
Shall we go and see him?"

"We'll have a great day out," he said.
"We'll meet Super Hero, we'll eat
burgers and we'll go on all the
scary rides!"
My Dad is very brave.

We woke up very early on Saturday.
We had a big breakfast.
Mum waved as we drove off to the
Fun Park.

As Dad drove, he told me about the scary rides. He told me all about the Ghost Train. "There are ghosts and vampires and mummies and bats and loud, creepy noises," said Dad in a creepy voice.

"That sounds really scary," I said.
"Oh, it's only a ride," said Dad.
"There's nothing to be scared of."

He told me all about the Roller-Coaster. "It goes whooshing down the hill and up again.

It goes round and round, faster and faster and faster!" said Dad in a whooshy voice.

"That sounds really scary," I said.
"Oh, it's only a ride," said Dad.
"There's nothing to be scared of."

He told me all about the Rocket Ride.
"It's a bit like watching a film,
but the spaceship moves.

You feel like you are flying
through space and the aliens are
trying to catch you!" said Dad in
an alien voice.

"That sounds really scary," I said.
"Oh, it's only a ride," said Dad.
"There's nothing to be scared of."
My Dad is very brave.

At the Fun Park,
we waited for
Super Hero.
We waited a
long time.

Then his car came and
Super Hero got out.
I couldn't believe it
was really him!

Super Hero shook my hand!
My tummy went all funny.
Super Hero smiled.

Then we went on the Ghost Train. We sat in a car and went through an old ghost house. It was full of spider webs and creaky doors.

There were ghosts and vampires
and mummies and bats and loud,
creepy noises.

Next we went on the Roller-Coaster.
We rolled slowly up a hill.
At the very top you could see the
whole Fun Park down below.
"Look, there's Super Hero!
He's waving at us, Dad!"

G-g-g-great!

Then we went whooshing down
the hill and whooshing up again.
We went up and down
and round and round,
faster and faster and faster!

When we got off the Roller-Coaster,
I had a great big burger and fries
and cola. Dad said he wasn't hungry.

Then we went on the Rocket Ride. We sat in a spaceship. It was a bit like watching a film, but the spaceship moved.

It went up and down, side to side,
backwards and forwards. It felt like
we were flying through space.
The aliens were trying to catch us!

On the way home, I told Dad
the bits that I liked best.
"I liked it when the spaceship
was being chased by aliens."
"That was great," said Dad.

"And it was fun meeting
Super Hero, wasn't it?" I said.
"That was my best bit," said Dad.

When we got home, I told Mum all about the Fun Park rides we had been on.

Mum couldn't believe that we had been on so many rides.

"Weren't you scared?" she asked.
Dad winked at me.

"Huh!" he said.
"Nothing scares us, does it?"
"Huh!" I said.
"Nothing scares us at all."

"Well," said Mum,
"you are *my* Super Heroes!"

Look out for more fun titles in the First Storybook series.

Super Dad *by Shoo Rayner*

My dad is a very busy dad. He doesn't always have time
to play with me. Then one day Super Hero comes to visit
and we have the best day ever. But Super Hero looks very
familiar. Perhaps my dad knows why – after all he *is* a
Super Dad!

Mulberry Home Alone *by Sally Grindley*

Mulberry the dog doesn't like being home alone. But he tries
to make the best of it. First he searches for his doggy crunchy
things. Whoops! He's knocked over the rubbish bin. Then
he decides to chase Cat. Whoops! He's crashed into the
telephone table. Luckily, Mulberry isn't home alone for long.

Mulberry Alone in the Park *by Sally Grindley*

The front door has been left open. It must be doggy
walkies time for Mulberry. So off he trots to the park. He
has great fun chasing squirrels and doggy-paddling after
the ducks. But then it starts to get dark. Mulberry is woken
by a loud bang, then another. Bright colours light up the
sky. Maybe being alone in the park is not such fun after all...

All these books and many more in the Storybook series can be
purchased from your local bookseller. For more information
about Storybooks, write to: *The Sales Department, Macdonald
Young Books, 61 Western Road, Hove, East Sussex BN3 1JD.*